BEYOND
THE ILLUMINATED SEA

BEYOND
THE ILLUMINATED SEA

Valy Marval

LES EDITIONS AMERICAINES

© LES EDITIONS AMERICAINES
2025

Library of Congress
ISBN 979-8-9907180-6-7
All rights reserved

Cover and text by Valy Marval

"I was shipwrecked without the slightest storm, in a sea where I had a foothold. "

Fernando Pessoa

"You can't find peace by running away from life..."

Virginia Wolf

"*The sea, that vast poem that whispers secrets to those who listen with their heart.*"

Gustave Flaubert

"Try always to keep a piece of heaven above your life. You have a beautiful soul, of a rare quality, don't let it lack what it needs."

Marcel Proust

*"... she possessed that natural quality of 'mystery'
which makes some women so good at hiding what
they lack, allowing men to guess all the virtues
they attribute to them...*

Romain Gary, Lady L.

To BBL, my beloved friend.

Where does the end of the sea begin? In the foamy waves that die at our feet, or in the voracious immensity that swallows everything without a sound?

One sea, one island.

Pangea, an original unity that has broken up over time, separating, drifting, nostalgia for a lost union.

"Thousands have lived without love. None have lived without water. "

The sentence had cracked like a whiplash in the warm night air, followed by the rustle of water as Stéphane's hand struck the surface with a theatrical gesture.

Around them, the pool stretched out, dark and quivering, bathed in the spotlights whose milky light cut the columns of steam into volutes.

The water smoked, exhaling its warmth into the night like a drowsy animal, and Judith, fascinated, followed with her eyes the mini tornadoes of mist that danced above them before disappearing.

She shivered slightly, but not from the cold.

This sentence had crossed her mind, with the trenchant simplicity of the obvious that we forget to face. Ninety-seven percent of the Earth's water sleeps in the oceans. A silent, patient immensity that contains all that has been and all that will be. As if, in the end, the world belonged to water far more than to those who try to survive in it.

She loved these moments, these suspended nights when the silence of the water enveloped them, when there was nothing but their bodies gliding beneath the surface, slow and precise, barely touching each other's skin before diving back in. Apnea was more than just a game. It was ecstasy.

A slow vertigo, a willing drift.

Hold the air, feel it swell your chest, then let yourself sink, dissolve in the water, forget your own weight, your own name.

Nothing existed anymore. Just this calm intoxication, this absolute freedom where the body no longer weighed anything and thought expanded, vast and limpid.

Stéphane was watching her, an imperceptible smile on his lips. She sensed him without seeing him, guessed the tension in his muscles under the trembling light.

There was something unsettling in the way he looked at her, a burning hesitation between provocation and desire.

A little further on, he could have kissed her. Here, it wasn't necessary. The water offered them another form of abandonment, another way of brushing against each other, of approaching the unspeakable.

She took a deep breath and dived in first.

The wave closed over her like a gentle hand.

The sea, immense, sovereign, before everything, after everything. Before us, after us. It was there when Pangaea broke up, splintering into continents, separating lands and peoples, tracing the world's borders.

Water has covered everything, shaped everything, sculpting shores as it sculpts souls, gently or furiously.

Maybe that's what love really is. An inner sea, shifting, unpredictable. A force that binds and separates, shapes and engulfs. A tide that overtakes us and carries us along, even when we think we're walking on solid ground.

But where does the land begin? Where does the sea end?

Perhaps there was never any separation. Just waves that come and go, like us, constantly moving backwards and forwards towards what we believe to be the other.

I passed a woman.

A dazzling woman who didn't seem to know she was.

She moved through life with that unconscious gentleness, that mixture of grace and awkwardness that makes some people unforgettable.

His weakness, or perhaps his greatest folly, was to love.

To love with an insane fervor, convinced that love could fix everything, redeem everything.

She believed in impulses, in miracles, in broken souls that can be glued back together with a little tenderness and a lot of patience.

She was wrong, of course. But that was precisely what made her so moving.

Arthur heard himself thinking these words without really formulating them, surprised to be reached at this point. It was as if, in understanding her, he was suddenly aware of everything he'd never been able to feel.

Unsettled, he climbed into the airport cab, concealing his confusion behind an implacable mechanic. His mind wavered, but his gestures remained surgically precise: door closed with a snap, belt buckled without hesitation, address given in a calm voice. Every action was a bulwark, an illusion of control against the inner chaos that threatened to overwhelm him.

The lights of the Place de l'Étoile faded behind him, swallowed up by the Parisian night.

Ahead, Sardinia awaited him, a distant promise, a softer horizon, where the tumult of his thoughts might find respite.

Judith watched the assembly with that mixture of amusement and weariness typical of long Parisian evenings, where rational intelligence triumphed noisily, while emotional intelligence died silently, suffocated under logical reasoning and demonstrations of ego.

The reception room at the Department of Culture resembled all reception rooms in public institutions: too large to be intimate, too impersonal to be grandiose. The architecture, though designed to impress, aroused nothing but polite boredom. Here, heroes without exploits were celebrated, careers honored more by habit than by merit. A ceremony without sparkle, where medals had become decorations without prestige, hung on jacket lapels by distracted hands, a ritual of entre-soi where everyone congratulated themselves on still being there.

The chandeliers, too strong, imposed their raw whiteness, drawing the shadows of time on the faces. They revealed, with an almost cruel brutality, incipient baldness, dark circles concealed under too much orange foundation, tired skin that no flattering light could soften. It was impossible to take a photo without a filter, without a quick correction to soften the harshness of reality. Judith hated these direct lights, not only because she was scotopic and could see in the dark like a cat, but above all because she knew that a simple ray of sunlight grazing a panel was enough to give relief to the world. Here, there were no nuances, no poetry: just a clinical, murderous whiteness that reduced everything to a flat surface.

The caterer was renowned, which didn't mean much. His amuse-bouches were like those honorary decorations: bland, conventional, designed to please no one rather than to seduce. Little stuffed puffs, vaguely exotic mini-brochettes, interchangeable verrines. Everything was easily eaten, without leaving a lasting impression.

And then there was the sparkling wine, that great lie served with a knowing smile. The Italians had won again: prosecco had replaced champagne.

Everyone pretended to appreciate it, under the guise of what was called "art of living", that magic word that justified all the shams. Officially, it was festive, sunny, almost Mediterranean.

Unofficially, it was a watered-down version of a greater emotion, a joyful simulacrum designed to be accessible. Judith could see the deception. The orange color of the beverage was insidiously influencing the brain, activating that cognitive bias that associated this hue with warmth, well-being, the Dolce Vita. But the bubbles, light and shallow, had none of the sparkle of champagne. They were merely an alibi.

Few men like champagne. It's women who love it, and rightly so. Mention the word "champagne" and a world immediately springs to mind: parties, music, love, grand declarations, victories, endless nights. It's Audrey Hepburn, cigarette at her fingertips, toasting in Diamonds on the Sofa; it's James Bond, casually telling the waitress: "Bollinger, if you have it. Otherwise, Dom Pérignon '52". It's Gatsby, watering his castle with promises and regrets, it's Cary Grant and Grace Kelly in *To Catch a Thief*, a glass in hand under the Riviera sky.

But no one has ever shouted "Prosecco!" and triggered a dream. There's no prosecco in the movies where we love each other, where we kiss at midnight, where we celebrate a victory that counts. There's prosecco on the terraces of crowded bars, at weddings where you're watching your budget, at receptions where you're pretending.

Judith swallowed a sip, under no illusions. There was no celebration or promise here. Just a shadow theater where everyone played their part, waiting for the curtain to fall.

María, fifty-five, a researcher at a renowned institute, divorced and nearing the end of her career, expounded with almost academic fervor the benefits of swinging parties as a last bastion of marital freedom. She spoke with a mechanical conviction, drained from a lifetime of searching for something she'd never found. Judith, her chin resting on her hand, gave an ironic look. This new fashion for belated transgression exasperated her.

The same individuals who had obeyed the dogmas of a well-oiled system all their lives, imposing rigid rules on others, were now getting down on all fours, bare-assed, in hushed salons, waiting to be grazed by anonymous hands.

They cooked their fish well to avoid parasites but offered their intimacy to strangers with an almost bureaucratic abandon.

An investment banker, Pierre, whose face still bore the remnants of a handsome face, recounted his professional and sentimental setbacks with theatrical solemnity. His divorce, his incompatibility with his colleagues... every ordeal became a performance in which his ego flourished even in complaint. Always grabbing attention, turning every exchange into a monologue, with the implicit certainty that her existence deserved to be listened to like a great epic. Judith smiled inwardly: failure became glory, a new way of being the hero of one's own story.

A handsome sailor, with the air of one who knows how to tame the wind and the sea, listened without saying a word. Women inevitably liked him. He embodied salt, horizon, independence. But Judith could recognize the emptiness behind his self-assurance. A man incapable of attachment, who thought he was free but was running away.

A childhood wound, no doubt, or perhaps simply the painful awareness of having been the family sportsman when his brothers were in the ministries.

Even his last crossing had been made possible by their contacts. He belonged to that category of beautiful people whose eyes tell another story: immense loneliness disguised as freedom.

The men in this room were touching. The women, infuriating. Or perhaps they were all exasperating.

There was talk of weekends in Europe, the Perche for the more rebellious, Corsica, but only if you had lunch in a picturesque port with a pastel Ralph Lauren shirt and a *"Grazie mille"* declaimed over the full vocal range.

Dominique and Isabelle, aged sixty, expatriates in the United States after a few years in Switzerland, worn-out executives of a large group, mentioned with hushed pride their three children who had become seaweed farmers in Thailand or surfers in Costa Rica.

They no longer saw them, of course, but consoled themselves by congratulating themselves on their independence. What they didn't know was that, under the guise of freedom, they'd taught them above all not to weave deep ties with anyone without involving money, power or success.

—

And then there was Camille, the artist with the overly colorful earrings and overly flowery skirts. She exhibited in galleries owned by her well-placed friends, created works that were more decorative than moving, and organized vernissages where everyone came to show off their traumas, camouflaged under tasteful outfits.

She belonged to a world of superlatives and tight timing: "I'm just out of an appointment", "I'm in a cab", "I've got a plane tomorrow". It was as if constant occupation had become a guarantee of importance.

Judith wondered if Arthur perceived all this. But he was, as always, far away, locked in his own thoughts, deaf to dissonance, insensitive to the subtleties of the moment. She thought of Schopenhauer's phrase: "The world in which a man lives depends less on what he sees than on what he thinks."

She sighed inwardly. Was she still hoping that Arthur would awaken to a different perception of the world? She might. Without much conviction.

"What you find in life is what you put into it". Paul Valéry and neuroscience would agree: the adult brain is difficult to remodel. And Arthur never put anything into the poetry of the present.

Dominique and Isabelle were a couple whose appearance fit the archetypal expatriate executive. Neither particularly handsome nor ungainly, they embodied what their milieu considered to be the ultimate: smooth faces, impeccable but unassuming clothes, and measured gestures that reflected self-control rather than real spontaneity.

They had that physical neutrality that allowed them to fit in anywhere without ever standing out. Dominique, with his salt-and-pepper hair cut short, wore a white linen shirt that was always freshly ironed, and well-cut jeans, chosen to be both casual and formal. Isabelle, her figure well-groomed but not overdone, preferred flowing blouses and cigarette pants, and wore the conventional smile of women who have spent too long in circles where conviviality is more a social game than a real pleasure.

Their posture was that of those who had learned to move within the codes of a certain class cosmopolitanism: the moderate tone, the ability to feign interest while maintaining a slight distance, a hushed refinement that was not embarrassed by outbursts or outbursts. They listened more than they spoke, gauging conversations to slip in with just the right amount of wit or detachment.

As for Pierre, the investment banker, he was the embodiment of the alpha male in decline. Always well-dressed, but his tired face revealed a daily battle against time, against sagging, against the inescapable. His gaze betrayed wear and tear rather than charisma, and his mouth twitched into a smile, testifying to an ego still struggling to keep its footing.

He spoke of his setbacks as a heroic tale, unable to perceive how his narcissism isolated him more than it enhanced him.

As for the navigator, he was seductive even before he opened his mouth. Tall, athletic, with that burnished complexion that women found irresistible, he could have embodied adventure, freedom.

But his eyes told a different story, that of a man unable to be there, always somewhere else, always on the run. He wasn't an adventurer; he was a permanent escapee. On closer inspection, everything about him reflected this dissonance: his physical assurance contrasted with gestures that were a little too mechanical, and a voice that was poised but lacking in any real depth. He appealed but left a taste of unfinished business.

Camille, the artist, was a caricature of herself. Her earrings were too colorful, her skirt too flowery, her gestures too studied to be truly bohemian.

She wanted to be vibrant, but her works were more decorative than subversive, and her art served more as a social prop than a sincere expression. When she did speak, she lined up hollow superlatives and overly enthusiastic adjectives, punctuating her sentences with falsely inspired sighs. Her agenda was overloaded, but she was chasing emptiness.

And then there were the others.

These men and women, all from the same backgrounds, convinced themselves that they embodied modernity when in fact they were its last vestiges. They spoke of sexual freedom at fifty, having spent their youth following the norms with discipline.

They ran to swingers' clubs like catching a missed train, convinced that this was, at last, the transgression that would add salt to their lives. They stood tall in their well-tailored suits and well-cut dresses, but as soon as you peeled them back a little, all that was left was an immense quest for sensation, a desperate attempt to feel something again.

Judith watched them, half-amused, half-jaded. She saw in them the reflection of an era on its last legs, of an entre-soi that went round in circles, always believing itself to be in the vanguard. And in this whirlwind of certainties and contradictions, she wondered if, deep down, she wasn't just as trapped as they were.

There are beings who make a sun in a room, wrote Victor Hugo.

This sentence seemed to have been written for this very moment. In this hushed, conventional world, where everything was staged without conviction, where bursts of laughter only served to mask boredom, there he was, standing in front of her, with that irresistible accent when he pronounced "Excuse me". An American. William.

His hazel-green eyes betrayed his Latin origins. His voice was frank, calm, serene and lively. Judith was taken aback. In this assembly where everything seemed frozen, where conversations resembled each other to the point of indistinction, there was an anomaly.

A burst of light. And, best of all, it had just spoken to her.

As she always did whenever she was taken aback, she chose to laugh. A joyful, flowery laugh that smelled of the beach, the sun and warm bodies.

He watched her, amused.

"How to stop partying and start laughing?"

It was with this phrase that he had approached her. As if he knew exactly where to touch her.

William had heard her talk about champagne and prosecco. He wasn't offended. Quite the contrary, in fact. He was the owner of the estate that supplied the reception, and he found this little Frenchwoman audacious enough to question an Italian jewel with such aplomb.

Her eyes said: I love you already.

"So, tell me, Judith, what do you have against prosecco?"

She smiled, amused.

"It's not so much that I have something against it, it's just that nobody dreams while shouting "Prosecco!" We dream by shouting "Champagne!".

"You're tough."

"Realistic. It's like the sea and the pool. We don't dream of diving into a pool, we dream of dashing into the salt water, feeling the swell, swimming until we can no longer see the shore."

William raised an eyebrow, intrigued.

"Do you swim in the sea?"

"As much as possible. It's my only real refuge."

"Me too."

A shiver ran down Judith's spine. That "me too" sounded different, like a secret promise, an intimate correspondence even before it was formulated. She watched him. His hazel-green gaze had that special depth of those who know the infinite horizon of the sea.

"There's something fascinating about the sea," he continues. "You get rid of the weight of your body, you float, you feel free..."

"And thoughts too," she added. "Sorrows remain on the surface, like an old fishing net left behind."

"Exactly. And then that feeling when you dive in, when the water engulfs every inch of skin, as if you were becoming something else again..."

"Almost a wave. Energy."

"Do you believe in energies?"

"I believe in vibrations. In that feeling of fullness when you swim far away, when the noise of the world disappears, when everything becomes silent and moving at the same time."

"You know what I love most? That moment when you're suspended between two waters, just before resurfacing."

"That moment when you almost forget you have to breathe?"

"The very one."

A silence stretched between them, but it wasn't awkward. It vibrated with an undertone, a beginning, a quiver. Judith, usually so ironic, so distant, felt her heart quicken slightly.

"Would you like to swim with me one day?" asked William with a wry smile.

She stared at him for a moment before answering, falsely casual:

"I don't mind. But only if you promise not to try to distance yourself from me."

"I never distance from who really swims."

"So we'll have to see if you can keep up."

And this time, it was his turn to laugh. A frank, clear laugh that echoed his own. Judith straightened slightly, tingling with excitement. She didn't believe in destiny, but she did believe in encounters that make you vibrate like a string stretched in the wind.

And something told him this was one of them.

"You know," she says, tilting her head, "swimming is a bit like art."

"Really?"

"It's a way of pruning away all that's unnecessary, getting back to the essentials. When you're in the water, all that's left is movement, breathing and momentum."

William smiled, his gaze gazing into hers as if he'd just found something rare.

"So, you believe that art and the sea can help us confront the absurdity of existence?"

"I'm convinced of it. When everything else seems to have lost its meaning, there are still those suspended moments when you feel alive."

He nodded thoughtfully.

"You may be the first person I've met who expresses so well what I've always felt."

She shrugged, playing it light.

"Or maybe you just hadn't yet met the right person to talk to about it."

A shiver passed between them, imperceptible but undeniable. Judith wondered if, after all, fate wasn't mocking her a little tonight.

They walked leisurely up the Rue Royale. The end-of-day light caught on the gilding of the fountains, gliding over the pale stone of the Madeleine. Everything looked more beautiful than it probably was, but that was the effect of twilight, or wine.

"It's not the one who thinks of you at dawn, alone in his bed, that counts," William let go.

Judith raised an eyebrow, amused.

"No?"

"No. He's the one who misses you at two o'clock in the afternoon, in the middle of a noisy café, laughing with friends and thinking, "*Merde*, I wish she was here."

He said this in a light, almost detached tone, but Judith felt the phrase catch somewhere inside her. And that "*Merde*" said in his American accent, a little too strongly, made her smile.

He was keen to prove that he had mastered the language, like a diligent student, and this simple detail, this will to do well, made it all strangely charming. They arrived at Concorde, the light melting stone and sky into the same soft, unreal gold.

"Because the other," says William, "is just a temporary void. And emptiness always seeks to fill itself, no matter with whom."

"Because the other one," continued William, "is just boredom. And boredom finds refuge in anyone."

Judith smiled, a wry smile, a little too silent. She already knew. But it was different when he was the one saying it.

Judith shut the Uber door, placed her bag beside her, and released a faint, nearly imperceptible sigh. The night had been tender and intimate. The driver, a man in his fifties with a face etched by the wear of too-brief nights and overly chatty passengers, cast a glance at her through the rearview mirror.

"Roissy?"

"Yes, Charles de Gaulle."

The car slipped smoothly through the streets, still holding the warmth of the prior evening. Paris was stirring into its signature mix of elegance and disorder. Judith cherished this fleeting hour, before the city surrendered fully to its indulgences.

The driver, by contrast, already seemed weary. With a tilt of his chin, he gestured toward yet another cyclist weaving unpredictably among the cars.

"Paris has turned into a mess. We used to gripe about traffic jams; now it's Russian roulette at every intersection. You see that, Madame? Those guys speeding down Avenue de Rivoli like it's a bike lane privatized by Hidalgo?

But it *is* a bike lane privatized by Paris Mayor Hidalgo."

He chuckled briefly.

"Exactly. We cabbies are survivors. Once we muttered about buses and tourists; now we weave between bikes, scooters, and Sunday joggers."

Judith smiled. She could picture precisely what he meant. Those Parisian bobos trotting along the quays in fluorescent headbands, faces bearing an air of urban martyrdom, as if atoning for their indulgent brunches with every strained step.

On Sunday mornings, it had become a secular ritual: legions in leggings, extolling the gospel of wellness between sips of detox juice.

"You know what amuses me?" she said, gazing out the window. "They run, they bike, they play at being free, yet they always stick to a straight line, neatly boxed in on their path.

Never a detour, never a spontaneous turn. They follow the markings like dutiful children."

The cabbie nodded.

"It's true, it's true. A neatly packaged freedom."

The car neared the Place de la Concorde. Judith gazed at the obelisk, the fountains, the refined gray of stone and sky. There was something elusive here, a whisper of the past enduring amid today's tumult. Paris could be strewn with plastic bollards and restricted lanes, yet she would always see the city as she had loved it: Saint-Germain at dawn, the muted patter of footsteps beneath the arcades of the Palais-Royal, the gleam of streetlamps on the Seine on a September evening. You could overlay the soul of Paris, alter its rhythms and routes, but something lingered. A melancholy, a weary yet unbroken majesty.

The driver eased to a stop before the terminal. He turned to her before she stepped out.

"You know, Madame... one day, folks like us, the quiet ones, will muster our courage and reclaim our city. Maybe not with barricades, but with memory.

With the way we stroll through Paris as if it still belonged to us."

Judith looked at him, caught off guard by this sudden reverie. Then she nodded slowly, offered a faint smile, and shut the door behind her.

Illusions, a game of appearances.

Sometimes happiness is hidden under a layer of doubt and fear.

Appearances are fragile illusions, facades that we adjust as circumstances dictate.

We're moved by those who collapse gracefully, we offer them a hand, a shoulder, an apology. But those who remain standing, wavering but proud, are ignored.

We'd rather look away than see what it costs to survive.

No one embraces the invisible wounds, no one collects the blood of those who are still moving forward. On must know how to suffer in silence, smile elegantly, and never ask to be looked at differently.

And then there are those days when you're not quite sure who owns your own life. Everything seems dictated by an outside force, a chain of choices we didn't really make.

We find ourselves playing a role we thought we knew, smiling out of habit, walking without knowing where we're going.

But tomorrow, everything will be different.

Because everything eventually dissipates, even the thickest mists, even fears carried for too long.

Appearances are delicate veneers, fleeting glints in the fickle glow of the world. We pardon those who stumble with grace, yet turn away from those who endure, scarred but upright despite it all.

Nothing endures—not fear, not even drifting.

Appearances are flimsy disguises, skins too frail to splinter in the stark light of day. Walking alone in stillness, while the world sweeps past without pause.

Judith ground her cigarette beneath the toe of her shoe, watching the smoke dissolve into the warm morning air, and let out a soft sigh. She wasn't so defiant after all.

It was simple to mock the bike-riding bobos and joggers entranced by their own reflections. Too simple. It had become almost a ritual, a tired instinct worn thin like a song played from memory, its lyrics unheard.

She shook her head. It was all familiar, too well-worn. What if *this* was the true snare? To stay trapped in a wry, cozy, but barren perspective. Like her life, her loves, her convictions—it all craved fresh momentum. Something new. A wider, clearer vision, free of pointless sarcasm, free of pretense, free of that mental fatigue that endlessly circled the same tired truths.

She yearned for something more. A way of thinking that wouldn't fracture, that wouldn't insist. A way of being that didn't merely react but created.

Huddled beside the ashtray, the precious remnants of spent tobacco awaited their destiny. A tramp, with a jeweler's patience, would gather them with his fingertips, crumbling them gently before tucking them into a stub he'd relight with a flicker snatched from the breeze. A treasure. His treasure.

Nearby, an old speaker crackled with a Julien Doré tune.

"We've been through Verlaine and Kafka, pour me some love in a glass of pastaga."

Irony, Judith mused, glancing at him from the corner of her eye. What if *this* was life?

A touch of love and a sunlit glass of pastis. A melody hanging in the morning air, scraps reclaimed and granted one final chance.

Judith observed the crowd in motion, the restless hum so characteristic of airports. Passengers scurried like ants, hauling overstuffed suitcases and transient dreams. Some strode swiftly, focused, as if their destination were already theirs to claim. Others drifted along, their movements steeped in routine, nearly sensing their gate before it appeared on the boards. A polished dance of hurried or detached souls, each bearing their own universe in their carry-on bags.

She paused for a moment. Because life wasn't here, in this ceaseless rush, this chase toward somewhere else. Life was in the tepid coffee cradled in her hands, in the light pouring through the vast window, in the raspy voice of a pilot announcing a delay with thinly veiled fatigue.

Returning to the joy of what we hold is a way of living, she thought. Not this frenzied pursuit of the next thing, not this mirage that more is always needed, always something beyond.

No, perhaps happiness rested in this quiet extravagance: knowing how to see, knowing how to feel, not striving to flee oneself at every turn.

She smiled as she reached for her ticket. Her flight had been called. And for once, she didn't feel like she was escaping.

One final glance toward Paris, then she turned away. It was time to leave.

Silence after another, after love, is perhaps the cruelest thing of all. It's not just the absence of a voice, a body, a habit that's missing. It's the absence of the witness.

Judith knew this. What she sometimes regretted wasn't her ex-husband, or even what they'd built together. A life for two, with its rituals, its concessions, its days of light and weariness. No, what hurt her most was that emptiness: not being looked at anymore.

No longer to be listened to, even distractedly. To no longer have this mirror, this imperfect but constant reflection that reminded her, every morning, that she existed in someone else's eyes.

That was it, a rupture. A camera turned off, a microphone cut off. No one to see her come home at night, to notice that she'd changed her perfume, to hear those tiny nuances in her voice that only habit can capture.

It was strange, this absence, this emptiness. Not so much the lack of a man, no, but the absence of that other gaze, that daily witness.

You don't share your life with someone just because they're pleasant, she told herself with a faint shrug. That would be too easy, too tepid. No, you share it because it rattles you and calms you in the same breath, because it can coax a laugh from you just as tears threaten to fall, because it maddens you as much as it captivates you. Because he sweeps you off your feet without ever holding you captive, because you ache for him even when he's near, and because his silences sometimes resonate deeper than his words.

And above all, because he's the only one who sees that your morning grumpiness is just shyness in disguise, that your cool aloofness is merely a shield.

But Judith no longer had that companion. No one to glance up from her phone and say, offhand, "That lipstick suits you." No one to tease her for always running late or to chuckle quietly when she bristled at the world. So she carried on.

Living, smiling, sparring with cabbies over Paris's decline, watching travelers drift through airports, trading bits of the past with fleeting strangers.

But sometimes, amid flashes of clarity, she wondered: was this truly the freedom she'd sought?

Or merely another shade of refined drifting?

For Judith, silence had long been a foe. A muted menace, a chasm poised to swallow her the moment the music faded, the voices hushed, and the night descended.

In the face of silence, the world contracts until it's a single pinpoint: oneself. And that point, if gazed at too long, can grow unbearable. She'd tried to evade it, like everyone else.

Filling her days with words, laughter, clamor, and melodies. Keeping her mind busy with facts, books, and tangled conversations. But silence was patient. It lingered, coiled beneath rehearsed phrases, in the pauses between lines. It always returned, steadfast and commanding, like the sea after a tempest.

Then one day, she ceased fleeing it. She realized it wasn't an emptiness, but a realm. A boundary where burdens could be set aside, where all that was trivial dissolved, leaving only what truly mattered. It was vertiginous. Raw. But utterly lucid.

Yet who, today, still dares to confront it? Who consents to sit in that silence without rushing to smother it with diversions and prattle? Perhaps that's why we hurl ourselves into the clamor, the screens, the loud assurances—because we dread what we might hear once nothing else remains.

With Arthur, it was another story. He wasn't a witness, nor had he ever tried to be. He lived alongside her, not through her. Perhaps that was why she felt unburdened in his presence.

And yet, at times, she longed for him to turn, to notice her silences, to sense that quiver of invisibility trembling beneath her skin. But Arthur wasn't that man. He gazed at the sea, at the night descending, at everything except her.

Judith revealed herself sparingly. You'd think you'd grasped her, only for her to slip away—like a shadow between two flickers of light—reappearing in a different guise, with a smile, a silence, a thought you hadn't known she held.

She resisted being pinned down, captured in a single frame. She was fluid, elusive, a breeze that shifts just as you think you've caught its course.

The one thing Arthur knew for certain about her was her love of laughter. Not just any laugh. The kind that startles, that rumbles, that dismantles walls.

The kind that erupts between two sentences and, without warning, turns into a frozen instant when you realize, amid the storm, how much you cherish being there, with that person. How effortless it feels, without even trying.

Arthur was the quintessential brilliant, willful business consultant—brimming with confidence, yet somehow still charming despite his rough edges.

A man who, after two marriages and some fifty lovers, had entered that curious phase where the ego begins to fracture under the weight of late reckonings.

At sixty, he wore weekend casual with a studied nonchalance: a cashmere sweater draped over his shoulders, impeccably tailored jeans hinting at a tailor's mastery of "careless chic," and pristine white sneakers—because a man like him never truly let disorder take root, not even on his footwear.

He thrived in a hybrid realm, one foot in politics—where he counseled prominent figures while staying safely in the shadows—and the other in the Parisian bougie scene, dining with publishers and filmmakers, ribbing them fondly while savoring their company. He'd toss out a Chateaubriand quote at a business dinner and dissect interest rates with a writer, never once seeming out of place.

Arthur had this insatiable urge to charm—not just for the thrill, but as a conditioned response, a lingering tic from a childhood wound that never quite faded. Like a boy who, denied a vital compliment at six, spent his life gathering admiring looks the way others amass Swiss watches.

No matter how many women he loved, left, or let slip from memory, he always craved a feminine presence nearby—not for their sake, but for his own, for that small jolt of certainty that he still mattered.

Generous, yes, but on his terms: lavish trips, fine dinners, signed books from authors he knew personally—tokens of his quiet sway. He knew how to delight, but not always how to hear.

And then there was this murky space, something unresolved in his way of loving. Not from a lack of heart, but from distraction. From habit, too. From the powerful man's syndrome of believing his mere presence sufficed.

He forgot to say "I love you, " not because he didn't feel it, but because he assumed it was understood.

He forgot to brush the neck of the woman he felt so at ease with, because his thoughts were already elsewhere—tangled in ambitions, late-blooming doubts, and that faint vertigo of aging, when you realize seduction isn't a given anymore but an art demanding a touch more care.

He embodied that paradox of seasoned men who've conquered all yet quietly wonder if they've overlooked what truly counts. So he jogged on the beach, touted sports as a balm for time's anxieties, laughed heartily at dinner parties, and pressed on, certain the next chapter would finally hand him what he'd chased without ever quite naming it.

Judith peered through the window, lost in the boundless blue stretching below. Sea and sky bled into a vague horizon, a hushed pledge of liberty.

In a few hours, she'd be in Sardinia. A few hours of pure, untainted joy.

There, between realms, in this metal shell adrift above the abyss, she felt an odd serenity. A pause in the relentless stream of daily life. An interlude where nothing held sway.

She recalled *The Myth of Sisyphus*, where Camus described a profound unease before a mute world, a search for meaning met only with life's unyielding silence. What if, after all, boarding a plane was a modern echo of Sisyphus?

We settle in, buckle up, observe fellow passengers with that peculiar, detached closeness. We know we'll share the same fate for a few hours, yet we'll likely never exchange a word.

A fleeting tribe, bound by a common path and a shared surrender to the whims of aerodynamics. Like Sisyphus with his rock, we all understand we'll descend again, that this flight won't carry us to some grand epiphany—just to another corner of the earth where the cycle resumes.

But for now, everything pauses.

Time hangs still. No one can touch us here. No calls, no pressing duties. Just a tranquil present, like a quiet refrain between two movements of life.

Judith savored this mirage of reprieve. The coffee in its paper cup always carried a hint of liberty, and the sleeping faces around her formed a gallery of portraits—absurd yet tender in their stillness.

The corporate attorney to her right, dozing with his mouth agape; the anxious couple murmuring softly; the flight attendant with her rehearsed smile.

A small human drama adrift above the clouds.

She smiled.

Judith had noticed her the moment she stepped aboard. A teenager, perhaps seventeen, seated two rows ahead, swiping through her phone with practiced indifference. An "almost woman," caught in that odd stretch where maturity is performed like a starring role in a movie whose script she still believes she commands.

She wore a Zara outfit, artfully picked to echo high-end labels: an oversized black blazer, a pleated miniskirt, and tall boots that might've strolled off a Fashion Week runway.

Her shoulder bag gleamed with a minimalist, faux-bold flair, and her perfume—a knockoff of a timeless scent—wafted around her like an early claim to autonomy. Her hair, impeccably smoothed yet faintly mussed for that "I'm not trying, though I spent an hour at the mirror" look, framed a face chiseled by TikTok contouring tutorials. Her makeup, cribbed from the influencers she followed devoutly, sharpened cheekbones she wouldn't shed for years—unaware she'd one day miss them.

But what caught Judith most was that gaze.

A gaze split between boredom and disdain, brimming with the unsettling poise of someone who thinks they've cracked life's code after surviving three epic heartbreaks—one with a boy who stopped replying on WhatsApp. A look that declared, "I'm beyond all this," certain the future was hers to claim, and that age would never catch up.

She surveyed the other passengers as relics of a bygone age, grown-ups outpaced by the times, fossils of a world she'd dismiss with a flick of her polished nails.

Judith smiled as she observed her. She, too, had once been seventeen, armed with an ironclad belief that the world would yield to her confidence. She, too, had worn that expression, that air of "I'll never stumble like they did." And then life took over from there. She wanted to tell her that no one outruns time, that those boots would soon give way to others, that the steely gaze would mellow, that the smug certainty of knowing it all would fade into the gentle grace of doubt.

But why bother?

At seventeen, you only hear what you choose to.

So, Judith left her to her illusions, simply enjoying the touching and slightly cruel spectacle of this youth in performance, so sure of itself, and yet so fragile beneath its armor of fake leather and provisional certainties.

If life didn't have any meaning, then we had to make our own, if only for the space of a flight.

You had to imagine Sisyphus happy.

Or, failing that, imagine a plane where everyone stops pretending to be busy and finally enjoys that perfect moment when nothing matters.

They had arrived together, on the same plane, but Judith had the impression that he had arrived later.

During the flight, they had exchanged a few words, shared a knowing smile, but there was this imperceptible distance, this slight gap, as if Arthur never really landed at the same moment as the others.

At the airport, he'd rented the car, taken the keys with his usual assurance, and on the way to their temporary refuge, he'd spoken to her in a calm, almost domestic tone. Listening to him give directions, commenting on the winding road lined with ancient olive trees, a stranger might have thought she was his wife.

He had this natural way of making the moment his own, of establishing an intimacy that felt like a commitment, but in his case, never was.

She moved through the house in stillness, grazing the phantoms of Arthur's life, and flung open the windows to the sea. The briny air stung her skin, stirring a memory older than she was.

The driftwood carried the scent of time, olive oil, and something elusive—a whisper of lives gone by.

The sun dipped toward the horizon over Sardinia. The private beach unfurled below, framed by rocks as smooth and rounded as human shoulders.

Golden light spilled across the landscape like a shroud of molten amber, wrapping everything in an ethereal softness. The sky, once a vivid blue, softened into a wash of pinks, oranges, and tender mauves—that fragile mauve that graces only summer evenings, when the day lingers in exquisite retreat.

The house's broad ochre stones seemed to radiate from within, releasing the warmth they'd gathered all day. Between the cracks in the walls, rosemary sprouted wild, releasing its potent, resinous, almost heady aroma, blending with the salt-laden mist drifting up from the sea.

The foliage, thick and alive in the gilded glow, trembled faintly, brushed by the warm breeze. Agaves stretched their pointed leaves like living statues, while the twisted olive trees cast long, graceful shadows over the grass.

The natural staircase, carved by wind and tide, twisted between the rocks down to the beach below. Its uneven steps, worn smooth by time, held the unseen traces of bare feet that had paused there, wavering between shore and sea.

Below, a handful of fishermen's boats— faded pastel shades of sky blue, sea green, and weathered white—rested on the sand. They looked abandoned there, like the final strokes of an impressionist canvas, gifted to the twilight's gaze.

At the end of the wooden dock, a lone figure stood etched against the light. A fisherman, still as stone, cast his line into the calm waters. He had the quiet endurance of those who understand the sea, and in that suspended glow, he seemed to hail from another era—a living Japanese print, where man and nature melded, steeped in the scent of rosemary and the boundless.

She slipped off her sandals, letting her feet meet the warm earth. She wanted to feel. She wanted to feel it all.

Arthur had vanished an hour after they arrived. He carried the air of someone who never asks for anything, gliding through the world without obvious faltering, yet bearing unseen fissures just beneath. His eyes were shadowed, laden with a past he wore like armor.

"Judith."

"Arthur."

No peck on the cheek. Just this tension, this unseen thread that tethered them together while holding them apart.

There it stood, perched on the cliff like a guarded secret. A house with sun-bleached sand shutters, weathered by salt and time, yet brimming with untold tales. Judith nudged the door open, and a warm, spiced breeze brushed her skin: the aroma of polished wood, aged linen, and sunlight steeped into the stones. And, faint, almost intangible, a wisp of feminine perfume lingered— a trace of the past that refused to fully dissolve.

She stepped into the wide room, where open windows framed a stunning sweep of the sea. Below, the private beach unfurled, bordered by pale rocks and silken sand. The air carried the scent of myrtle and mastic—wild, heady, almost visceral.

Farther off, fig trees sagged under their ripe bounty, heavy and sweet, some splitting in the heat with a faint pop, a quiet gift surrendered to the breeze.

Everything here beckoned to the senses: the stark light carving every contour, the pulsing chant of cicadas, the warm breeze skimming her skin like an unbidden touch. But Judith wasn't deceived. She knew a place's beauty could be a mirage; a lavish façade masking unseen fractures.

That's when she spotted him.

Arthur leaned against the staircase railing, watching her in silence. A suspended instant, heavy with a quiet, familiar strain.

"You're here," he murmured at last.

"Yes."

She set her suitcase in a corner. He didn't stir to assist her. It was a ritual between them: a deliberate distance, a dance with rules they both understood.

She scanned the room. The photos remained. Black-and-white snapshots, pinned up haphazardly. A woman's face, laughter caught in time, a familiar outline.

Arthur's ex-wife.

A ghostly presence that quietly asserted itself, whispering that this house didn't just belong to the present.

Arthur approached and Judith sensed a slight hesitation in his movement, as if he wanted to say something to her but didn't know where to start. Finally, he simply poured two glasses of white wine, cool and mineral.

"I'll take them off," he says, pointing to the photos.

"No."

She was lying. But she wasn't ready to admit it, even to herself.

He sat on the sofa, staring out to sea.

"You know, Judith... sometimes I wonder if love isn't a series of echoes. Voices from the past echoing in those of the present.

She took a sip of wine. Her heart tightened slightly.

"I'm not the one to ask."

He stared at her for a moment, then looked away.

She knew that look. That of a man fighting against his own shadows but who hadn't yet decided to face them.

Here she stood, in this house, on this island drenched in light. She could feel every thrum of nature around her, every gust of wind against her skin. She was alive, electric.

But was she merely a woman to him tonight, or just a shadow, a patient listener into whom he could pour his secrets without risk?

A memory of Frida Kahlo surfaced: *"If I have to ask you, I don't want it anymore."*

The words coiled around her like a truth she wasn't ready to confront. If she had to beg to be seen in his eyes, then she didn't want it.

The island pulsed with life. The vegetation, thick and bold, exhaled its perfume. The rich scent of ripe fig trees swelled in the heat. Judith swam early, before Arthur stirred. The water enveloped her, soothed her, washed away what she'd thought permanent.

The sun draped itself languidly over her skin, cloaking her in a silken, almost fluid warmth, like a sheet kissed by summer.

Across from her, the sea rolled out its timeless breath, stark and mesmerizing, a deep blue laced with glints of gold. The air carried salt, wild herbs, and the intoxicating scent of the Sardinian maquis—a fusion of myrtle and rosemary clinging to the sun-scorched stones. She let the breeze brush her face, warm and aromatic, while far off, along the shore of Santa Teresa, a handful of fishermen readied their nets in the faint shade of their grounded boats.

"Sometimes, to love is to embrace imperfection and let yourself be uncovered, " she murmured, more to herself than to Nicolas, her childhood friend stopping by the island, who'd joined her briefly before heading back to his restaurant.

He chuckled quietly, his form outlined against the vivid blue of the sea. Having roamed the globe at the whims of a billionaire obsessed with fine dining and rare finds, he'd risen to become a celebrated chef, yet here he was the boy of old again, the one who dreamed while gazing at the waves.

"It's all about vibrations " he said, settling beside her. "Everything's energy, everything's motion. When you cook, you sense the pulse of the ingredients—their story, their melody. Look at the sea: that's all it does—vibrate, beckon."

Judith nodded, her eyes half-shut. She recalled a tale from an old Sardinian fisherman: the sea lifts those who heed its voice. He'd said water echoes inside us, like sand mandalas swept away by the breeze, like the humming tones of Tibetan bowls stirring something long dormant within.

Nicolas offered her a plate—simple yet striking—bearing a serving of *zuppa gallurese*, the region's ancient dish, modest yet hearty: bread steeped in aromatic broth, softened beneath a blanket of pecorino and wild mint. She took a bite, tasting anew all this land held: the bite of the winds, the gentleness of the cheese, the comfort of shared bread.

"Cooking's like love," Nicolas said. "It takes patience, precision, and the grace to accept nothing's flawless. "

Judith smiled. The flavor of melted cheese lingered on her tongue, a quiet vow of something vital. The vital, perhaps, was right there: in the salt on her skin, in the shimmer of sun on the water, in this fleeting exchange bridging childhood and what lay ahead.

Judith tilted her head up, a playful smile curling the edge of her lips. She fixed Nicolas with that sly spark that always heralded a sharp quip.

"Tell me, oh grand maestro of the world's tastes and enigmas, did you know mandala patterns are really the shape of a sound? Each vibration crafts a distinct form. Pure kinetics."

Nicolas arched an eyebrow, entertained.

"So, if I hum off-key, I'll whip up a lopsided mandala?"

"Precisely! Cosmic havoc in one sour note, " she teased. "Imagine the sea, with all its frequencies. It's got to be sketching a constant masterpiece, while we mere mortals fumble to decode it with our puny little minds."

He shook his head and chuckled.

"And you reckon your voice has already spun a flawless mandala?"

Judith narrowed her eyes, mock indignation flaring.

"Naturally. Every laugh of mine traces a golden one."

They erupted into laughter together, the ceaseless sea humming around them.

Nicolas looked at Judith, seized by a sudden, almost absurd urge to grab her hand and say, "Come on, I'll handle it all," like in some cheesy romance flick where no one's too bruised or too wary. But instead, he did what men do when they waver: he asked a question.

Judith raised an eyebrow, amused. She pretended to think, when in fact she knew exactly what she was going to say.

"What do you like in others? "

"A blend of charm and intelligence, goodness."

She paused to light a cigarette, savoring the small ceremony of the gesture.

"I like harmony and complicity. But above all, tenderness. That's when true intelligence is tested. I agree with Sagan. I'm all for progress in the charm of life. "

Nicolas smiled. He liked the way she put things simply, with a false casualness that concealed a sharp lucidity.

"So, if I understand correctly, brilliant but insensitive people are condemned to idiocy?"

"Exactly," she confirmed, blowing out her smoke. Like men who want to manage everything, but never their emotions.

He laughed softly. He didn't know if she meant him, but it was quite possible.

She could feel Arthur watching her from the terrace. He wasn't saying anything. But she knew.

The weight of uncertainty. The conviction of words. Rebuilding your life

"Judith, shall we go? "

"I adore when you seize control of my life, Arthur," she murmured, her tone laced with irony.

They strolled to the next village, picking up white wine, fish, and lemons. They cooked in quiet, their movements a blend of old familiarity and fresh closeness. The music looped—jazz, sonatas, an Italian tune she didn't recognize but that tugged at her heart.

"We've been pretending too long, Arthur." He glanced up. He understood.

"To the sea. To its false calm."

Light stretched languidly through the wide windows, casting shifting glimmers of the sea onto the walls.

Everything here felt brushed in watercolor: the fluid blue of the sky bled into the deeper teal of the water, and on the horizon, the waves lapped with a misleading softness. From this vantage, the sea was a vow of peace, a slow, even breath, as if the world had settled into balance.

But Judith knew it was a façade. The tempests churned beneath. Unseen. Perilous. Like within her, like within him.

Arthur had lingered by the bay window for a while, a cup of tepid coffee in his hands. He stared at the sea but didn't truly see it. Judith observed him in silence, sensing the shadows behind his eyes, those discords he bore like an unresolved tune.

She set her book aside and drew near.

"What's on your mind?"

He gave a fleeting, almost wry smile. She nodded.

"You know, one thing captivates me about the great painters. They never render a sea perfectly still. There's always a tension in the waves, even in the calmest seascapes. As if nature rejects absolute quiet. "

Arthur tilted his head slightly toward her.

"And music?"

"The same. Silences brim with life. You might think a piece is gentle but listen closely— there's always something beneath. A strain, a note hanging in the air."

He held her gaze for a beat, and she felt it again: that unseen barrier, the wall he always raised between himself and the world.

"You see, Arthur, wounds are like that too. Ignore them, and they don't vanish. They just shape how you move, how you speak, how you love."

She rested a gentle hand on his arm.

"Women feel it. They sense that absence, even when you're right there."

He looked away, down at the floor.

Judith sighed and stepped back. She didn't want a love stitched from half-presences, thick silences, and muted feelings. She craved a sea in motion, a melody where dissonance wasn't hushed but embraced.

She swung open the French doors and stepped onto the terrace. The sea air bore the tang of pine and salt. Beyond, the water gleamed, alive and untamed.

She shut her eyes for a moment.

Perhaps this was what it meant to love again after love: not striving to calm the waves but mastering how to crest them.

The wine had rinsed their spirits clean—or at least what lingered after a day brimming with unspoken pauses. Barry White's rich, velvet voice swathed the room in a soft haze, an unseen touch that skimmed the skin and sank into the pores. The bass thrummed deep, beneath the surface, pulsing in the chest—a tide that swelled and crashed within before dissolving into the body. Forty hertz of comforting allure, a vow from a realm where nothing ever feels too grave. *"I don't want clever conversation; I just want the way you are."*

Judith trembled, not from chill, but from that rare magic certain songs conjure: the sense that the universe hums on a single chord, as if this moment had already played out somewhere else, in a loop where time shrugs off its usual reign.

A fleeting, perfect harmony, delicate and rare, like the flicker of an eyelash you'd only wished could linger.

Arthur was already somewhere else. Absorbed in this elsewhere that he wore all the time, a prefabricated refuge where he carefully avoided anything that could reach him. He sipped his drink with that vaguely absent nonchalance she knew by heart, that slight crease in his forehead that meant he was thinking about everything but what was happening in front of him.

"Most of the time, I don't understand a word you say," he finally blurts out, almost distractedly.

Judith smiled that slightly mocking smile she reserved for men who were tired of themselves.

"It doesn't matter," she replies. "You feel, that's the main thing."

Judith could have laughed, shrugged her shoulders, poked him in the eye to cover up the old disappointment he had been feeding her like a catchphrase. But tonight, the effect was different, more pernicious. She thought back to Frida Kahlo's phrase: "*If I have to ask, I don't want to.*"

Arthur constantly provoked this feeling in her. Like a throbbing echo, a fine blade that barely nicked, just enough to sting without drawing blood. Sometimes, the urge to plant him there, without a word, without turning around, took her violently, like vertigo. A delicious, bitter temptation to leave him in his thoughts, facing the emptiness he refused to see, and dance away to Barry White, glass still in hand, without a backward glance.

Just to see if he'd trail after her. Just to see if, this once, he'd truly hear.

Barry White's warm, steady voice filled the air like an unseen stroke, the bass humming at 40 hertz—a quiet signal to the body, a ripple that flowed from skin to bone, stirring a faint tremor. Judith knew certain frequencies brushed against uncharted corners of the soul. But Arthur? He only skimmed the surface.

Her gaze slid over him, settled snugly in the cocoon of his inner realm. He retreated into his mind, favoring detachment over presence. He heard without listening, replied without engaging. Judith's smile carried no warmth.

He excelled at that: shrinking the vital into the mundane, sidestepping anything that demanded a hint of daring.

They met on the beach.

"I've spent my life not believing, Judith."

"Believing what?"

"That we can love again after love."

She smiled. Some wounds couldn't be mended—just fragments we learned to carry in new ways.

"You know, Arthur, I've been mulling something over," she said, folding her arms with a faint grin. "You should try *kintsugi*."

He arched an eyebrow, distracted, already half adrift.

"What's that?"

"*Kintsugi*! The Japanese art of mending broken things with gold. They say it makes them even more precious."

She let the words linger, her gaze drifting to the waves twitching faintly in the distance, as if they, too, had been shattered and stitched back together by some unseen thread.

"It's a lovely notion, don't you think?" she went on. "Far from worshipping perfection, the new, the unblemished. You embrace the fracture—not to hide it, but to highlight it. You trace the exact spot where the piece broke, not as a flaw, but as a testament to its story."

Arthur glanced at her sidelong, silent.

"You see, in our world, anything cracked gets tossed aside. Hearts, loves, weary souls. But with *kintsugi,* you don't cover the scar—you gild it. It's a way to honor what's been hurt, to say: here it is, there was a break, a tumble, and yet it endures. Maybe even more beautiful than before."

She spun her glass between her fingers, relishing the heft of her own words.

"It's an act of humility, too. Accepting we're not untouched. That we all carry scars, cracks where the light seeps through, like Cohen said."

Arthur flashed a brief smile, but his eyes had already strayed elsewhere. She knew him too well. He could hear, sure, but he wasn't truly listening. Always that distance, that knack for being there without ever fully giving himself over. She sighed, a mix of amusement and fatigue.

"Well, you, I suppose, if you took up *kintsugi*, you'd swap gold for platinum."

Arthur smiled faintly, nodded absently, his gaze drifting toward the horizon, snagged by some grander, weightier notion.

"It wouldn't hurt you," she pressed, feigning a thoughtful tone. "Patch up your cracks with a little shine. A philosophical facelift, if you will."

He chuckled softly, offering no reply, his eyes locked on the far-off line of sea and sky.

"But then," she added with a shrug, "men like you never heed the ones who know you too well. Too caught up plotting the next fight, the next prize, the next step."

She took a sip from her glass and sighed, mockingly nonchalant.

"And, between us, I doubt gold's enough to mend it all. Some pieces just end up dangling like mismatched trinkets."

Arthur didn't respond, but she knew he'd caught her words. She knew it better than anyone.

The sea, constant yet ever shifting, sprawled before them. Judith traced the ebb and flow of the waves with her eyes—the way they brushed the shore before pulling back, like a love that offers and withdraws. She thought of her marriage. Forty years. A lifetime. But now? She'd given everything. Her love, her body, her strength. She'd trusted in the certainty of things well built, in feelings that sustained themselves, in vows honored without strain. And yet, one morning, she awoke alone.

Love has an odd way of refining people. When you truly love, you don't just see someone— you see a mirror of your deepest yearnings and dreams. The other becomes a canvas for your light, and in that glow, they gleam. She'd done it. She'd done it her whole life. She'd lit up a man, never noticing that in the shadows, he was drifting into a stranger.

Because that's how it works: as long as you like it, you fix the image, smooth out the rough edges, minimize what makes you suffer.

But once the light fades, once the emotion subsides, the contours become clearer, the angles sharper, the silences heavier.

She had believed that the power to love was enough. That it was a bulwark against everything. She'd been wrong.

"What's on your mind? "

Arthur had just broken the silence. He had moved closer, his gaze resting on her with unusual gentleness.

"To what you do when you have to start all over again," she murmured."

He nodded.

"And did you find an answer?"

She rolled her glass between her fingers.

"Maybe we don't do it again. We just keep going."

Arthur didn't answer immediately. He stared at the sea, as if searching in its eddies for a truth greater than himself.

"Do you think it's possible to love after love?"

Judith smiled, a sad, lucid smile.

"Above all, I believe women don't get the luxury of not trying. "

Because beyond the sorrow, the solitude, and the scars, there was this stark truth: women have always had to remake themselves. They bear love like a duty, pouring their strength, patience, and endurance into it. They give, over and over, sometimes until they're spent. And when love departs, they're the ones left standing. Gathering the shards. Pressing forward.

That's what men don't always grasp. They think leaving or being left is the finish line. But for women, it's never the end. It's a metamorphosis. They don't have a choice.

Arthur watched her in silence. She knew his thoughts had drifted to his ex-wife, to the house where he'd loved her, to all those years when she'd been his certainty. But what he didn't see—or wouldn't—was that women couldn't afford the indulgence of static remorse. They didn't have the privilege of staying locked in a faded yesterday.

They had to rise anew.

"Judith…" He faltered.

She rested a gentle hand on his arm.

"Don't say anything. Tonight, it's not about what's gone."

Arthur nodded slowly. He raised his glass.

"To what comes next, then. "

She clinked her glass with his, her eyes still fixed on the sea. The sea erases nothing. It smooths, it reshapes, it renews. Judith, too.

When he placed his hand on her, it wasn't a claim or a triumph. It was tenderness after the tempest.

His fingers glided gently over her skin, tracing unseen paths, as if he sought to guide her through touch—to hold her without binding her. In that motion lay the weight of late-found truths, the depth of embraces where desire no longer flares wildly but smolders richly.

He touched her first, palm resting on her hip, then slowly rose, his lips grazing the arc of her shoulder. She trembled, not from haste, but from that quiet knowing of souls that meet and answer one another.

With his fingertips, he traced the curve of her spine, as if to root it within him, to etch it beneath her skin.

He leaned closer, his warm breath teasing the nape of her neck, and she arched faintly, yielding to this unhurried reunion. Their skin spoke an old tongue, a murmur of recognition. Nothing harsh, nothing reckless—just a clarity that took its time.

Judith stirred awake alone. Arthur had slipped out for his beach run, as he always did. He'd return.

She sipped her coffee, watching him recede—his form steady and purposeful, carving a track in the sand like a monk chasing wisdom. She knew the pattern. Men past fifty who ran like it was a chant, certain each step pushed back the unavoidable. As if age, weariness, and time were foes to be outpaced with the newest running shoes.

She didn't mind sports, naturally. But she'd clocked this odd zeal in some. A way of proclaiming "I'm running" with the same weight one might say "I'm meditating" or "I'm on a silent retreat in Tibet." The exertion turned into a creed, a statement of being.

"You should try it—it changes everything," a friend had once urged her, brimming with the fervor of the newly devout.

Change everything? Did it? Was that the secret to happiness after fifty? Slip on some shorts, punish your knees, and await enlightenment between twinges?

And then there was this wry twist: the same men who, two decades back, chuckled at those fussing over their physiques—finding calorie-counting or running without a bear on their heels absurd—now boasted their splits on apps, dissected their jogs like a Proust passage, and cast a faintly smug pity on the uninitiated.

Judith opted out. Not from stubbornness, but from plain clarity. She'd never bought into cure-alls. Running, sipping celery juice, striking yoga poses at sunrise, or dancing till collapse in clubs—all strands of the same mirage: that the body could stand in for inner reckoning.

She gazed at the sea. She, at least, had nothing to prove.

Arthur would trudge back eventually, winded but smug, with that glint in his eye—a cocktail of pride and self-vindication. And he'd say, as he always did:

"You should give it a shot, Judith. It might do you good."

And as always, she'd smile, handing him a coffee, relishing the quiet joy of not chasing the pointless.

But this morning, as she watched him return, her breath still ragged, her skin beaded with sweat, Judith let her thoughts drift elsewhere.

To a different kind of exercise.

A more sensible, livelier, truer sport.

She imagined for a moment their bodies entwined on the terrace, the warmth of the wood beneath her palms, her fingers gripping the railing polished by salt and wind. Arthur behind her, holding her firmly, his hands exploring her curves with that controlled slowness that makes desire last, that digs into it, that stretches it like a wave ready to break.

She could almost feel his breath on the back of her neck, the way he would have kissed her right there, on the birth of the shoulder, where the skin immediately tingles, where a simple touch can be enough to make the whole body capsize.

And the sea below, beating the rocks with the same cadence, like a natural echo to their movements. A primordial, instinctive dance. A perfect harmony between the crash of the waves and the tension of their loins, the inexorable rise of pleasure matching the roar of the foam.

She imagined the gentle bite of his fingers on her hips, the pressure of his lips against her burning skin, the way he would take her, slowly at first, then with the urgency that arises when two souls finally recognize each other, when the body no longer lies, when the moment becomes absolute.

A suspended, timeless present.

A love that no longer seeks to justify anything, that asks for no promises or future, just raw, visceral truth, offered unvarnished, undefended.

She blinked.

Arthur had just settled across from her, shirtless, sweat still beading from his run. He grinned, clearly pleased with himself.

"You should try it, Judith. It might do you good."

She held his gaze for a beat, a playful spark dancing in her eyes, still tangled in her own musings.

She lifted her cup to her lips, letting the silence hover between them before replying, a faint smile tugging at her mouth:

"Oh, you know, I already got my workout in this morning."

He arched an eyebrow, curious. But she offered nothing more. Some pleasures couldn't be pursued. They had to be relished.

She sipped her coffee, watching the sea—its shifting glints, its knack for being ever the same yet always new. Some loves blaze; others reshape. She didn't yet know which theirs was.

But she knew fear no longer held her.

"You know, Arthur, there are moments when it all blurs. It's not quite the life it was, nor something entirely new. It's neither false nor true—just time slipping by. That's all it is."

She said it lightly, almost offhand, but she knew he'd catch the undertone.

Judith never cared for overblown theatrics; she favored simple phrases—ones that skim the surface yet leave an imprint.

"Sometimes I feel caught between two realms," she went on. "Like I'm crossing a bridge with no end, unsure what lies beyond."

She took a puff from her cigarette, her eyes tracing the sea unfurling before them. Then she turned to Arthur.

"And you? Do you gaze into the water or leap in headfirst?"

He offered a faint smile, not answering right away. She knew he might not at all. Arthur had a knack for listening without wading in, letting silences stand in for words.

But Judith didn't need a reply. She just wanted to sense he was there, even wordlessly.

She fixed her gaze on the horizon, a subtle smile playing at her lips, then continued, her voice soft and almost wistful:

"The sea swallows ships and yields treasures. It doesn't hand out answers, Arthur, but it knows how to wait. It's an ancient soul—wiser than us, gentler, fiercer, wilder too."

She crushed her cigarette slowly, as if punctuating a thought. The breeze lifted a few strands of her hair, and she let them settle without a glance.

"But above all, the sea calls, you know. That's all it does: call. Relentlessly. You think you're watching it, marveling at it, crossing it—but it's crossing you. It seeps in and never lets go. You can pretend not to hear, but it's no use. It…"

"…will continue."

She turned to him at last, her eyes diving into his, a moment deeper than the expanse before them.

"That sea, and all the others you won't see but will feel anyway. There'll always be a sea calling you, Arthur. Just listen."

There was a strange sky for those who race, who charge full tilt—

"Fall backward, Arthur. Flinch. Be ready to plunge into an ocean of joy.

Happiness…

Be the presence! Be one with life! Be the infinite! Be the sea!"

ISBN 979-8-9907180-6-7
United States of America
© LES EDITIONS AMERICAINES 2025

www.ingramcontent.com/pod-product-compliance
Lightning Source LLC
Chambersburg PA
CBHW051146020726
47501CB00005B/1700